UNDER THE SKY OF
GAZA

MANAR SAMIR

تحت سماء غزة

بقلم: منار سمير

ISBN Print copy: 978-1-916814-99-8

ISBN Ebook: 978-1-916814-98-1

Cover image by Laurence Meehan

Dedication

To Gaza... to my family and my loved ones...
You are the story that never dies, the light that never fades no matter
how deep the darkness grows.

الإهداء

···إلى أهلي وأحبتي ···إلى غزة
أنتم الحكاية التي لا تموت، والنور الذي لا ينطفئ مهما اشتد الظلام.

A note from the author

The author of this short story is Manar Samir, born in 1996 in the Gaza Strip, Palestinian nationality, living under genocide, hunger and bombing, along with her daughter and husband:

"I wrote this while crying with hunger and crying with fear for my only daughter, Marseille. I hope you like it."

مؤلف الرواية منار سمير مواليد ١٩٩٦ مواليد قطاع غزة جنسية فلسطينية تعيش تحت الإبادة والجوع والقصف هي وطفلتها وزوجها كتبت هذا الرواية وانا ابكي جائعه وابكي خوفا على طفلتي الوحيدة مرسيليا اتمنى ان تنال اعجابكم

A Note from the Publisher

This short story was written by Manar Samir during the occupation of Gaza. She asked for help in producing this story through the Gaza Volunteer Hub, and I offered to format the book and prepare it for publication. At that time, I had not expected that I would also need to publish it for her, but here we are. The story is exactly as Manar sent it to me, with both her original Arabic version and the English translation she sent me through our chats on WhatsApp. All proceeds from the sales of this story will benefit Manar and her family directly, and provide crucial financial support for them to buy food, shelter, and other necessities — a literal lifeline. We hope you buy the story to offer your solidarity and support, but we also hope you enjoy it.

Thank you, your support means everything to the people of Gaza.

Jinny Alexander

Chapter 1
Childhood of the Sea

Adam was a boy unlike other children. While his peers were busy chasing after a ball or climbing the walls of houses, he would sit by the seashore, watching the waves come and go, as if they carried a secret far older than his young age.

His mother always told him: "Adam, the sea only reveals its secrets to those who are patient enough to listen."

And so he listened... listened for so long that he sometimes felt the waves were calling his name.

From an early age, he loved writing—scribbling incomprehensible words on scraps of paper, or drawing lines he imagined to be letters. As he grew older, he began recording his thoughts in an old notebook inherited from his father, a notebook that would later become his dearest friend.

On many nights, when the electricity was cut off and houses sank into total darkness, he would light a small candle and sit by the window. He was never afraid of the dark; instead, he saw it as a vast canvas upon which he could write whatever his imagination desired.

One night he wrote: "They may turn off our lights, but no one can extinguish the dream."

Adam grew up seeing his city under siege, hearing the sound of planes before he slept, and sometimes waking up to the news of losing a neighbor or a relative. Yet, the sea remained his safe haven. He would go to it whenever life became too heavy, pouring his sorrows into its waters and returning with a temporary calm, as though he had washed his soul clean.

Chapter 2

The Encounter

One summer day, while walking through the crowded marketplace, he noticed a girl standing in a small corner selling second-hand books. He approached, and his eyes fell on a book titled: "When Hearts Live Despite the Pain."

He smiled and asked her: "Is this your book?"

She smiled shyly and replied: "I wish I were the author... but it resembles me, for I live with pain while searching for life between the lines."

Her name was Salma, a girl about his age, with eyes that carried both sorrow and determination. From that day on, they met more often, talking about books and dreams. Each meeting became a window of light amid the darkness.

Chapter 3

Under the Siege

Their friendship grew quickly. They would sit by the sea for hours—she would speak of her dream of becoming a famous writer, and he would tell her about his notebooks filled with stories.

But the siege was present in every detail: electricity outages, water shortages, the constant hum of planes.

Salma used to say: "We live between two bombings, and yet we try to create a life in between."

Adam would smile and reply: "Then we are stronger than death, because we choose to love despite everything."

Chapter 4
The Beginnings of Love

As time passed, their meetings became more than just discussions about books. Something deeper grew between them—long glances, warm silences, and hearts that beat despite the fear.

Adam wrote in his notebook: *Every time I meet her, I feel I come closer to myself. She is not only Salma... she is the life I have been searching for.*

Chapter 5
The Storm

But in Gaza, peace never lasts long. One night, the sounds of explosions shook the city, and the sky ignited with fire.

Adam ran towards Salma's house after the bombing, but all he found was rubble and smoke. He searched for her in hospitals, among the faces of survivors, but she was nowhere to be found.

All that remained was a small notebook that had fallen among the ruins. With trembling hands, he opened it and found on the last page a line she had written: *If we cannot find life on this earth, perhaps we will find it within words.*

Chapter 6
The Search

Adam did not give up. For many days, he kept asking about her everywhere: at her relatives' homes, in hospitals, at relief centers.

Every answer deepened his fear, yet his heart refused to believe she was gone.

He wrote in his notebook: *I will search for you, Salma, even among the clouds and the smoke. You were never just a passerby—you were the homeland itself.*

Chapter 7
The Notebook's Letters

When he returned to the sea, Adam opened Salma's notebook and began to read her letters. He discovered it was filled with lines she had written but never shown him:

Adam, you were my friend when I needed one, my hope when I despaired, and I know that my words will reach you even if we are apart.

Every sentence was like a new heartbeat within him. He felt that Salma had not died, but was alive in her words.

Chapter 8
Hope and Writing

Adam sat by the sea, where everything had begun, but this time he was not sad. He held his pen and began writing his first novel.

He wrote about the sea that taught him patience, about Salma who taught him love, about Gaza that taught him resistance through life before weapons.

When he finished, he closed his notebook and said, "Stories will never fade as long as there are those who write them."

Then he lifted his eyes to the sky, which despite the clouds, still promised the birth of a new sun.

Epilogue

Under the Sky of Gaza, love is born despite death, and words remain when everything else is gone.

الفصل الأول: طفولة البحر

كان آدم طفلاً لا يشبه بقية الأطفال. بينما ينشغل أقرانه بالركض خلف الكرة أو تسلق جدران البيوت، كان
يجلس على شاطئ البحر، يراقب الموجة وهي تأتي وتعود، كأنها تحمل سرًّا أكبر من عمره الصغير.

أمه كانت تقول له دائمًا:
- "آدم، البحر لا يبوح بأسراره إلا لمن يصبر على الإصغاء".
يصغي طويلاً حتى يخيل له أن الموج يناديه باسمه ٠٠٠وكان يصغي.

منذ صغره أحب الكتابة، يخطّ كلمات غير مفهومة على قصاصات ورق، أو يرسم خطوطًا يظنها حروفًا. وحين كبر قليلاً، صار يدوّن يومياته في دفتر قديم ورثه من أبيه، ذلك الدفتر الذي سيصبح فيما بعد أعزّ أصدقائه.

في ليالٍ كثيرة، حين ينقطع التيار الكهربائي وتغرق البيوت في ظلام دامس، كان يشعل شمعة صغيرة ويجلس بجوار النافذة. لم يكن يخاف من الظلام، بل كان يعتبره لوحة واسعة يمكن أن يكتب عليها ما يشاء بخياله. كتب مرة:
"ربما يطفئون أنوارنا، لكن لا أحد يستطيع أن يطفئ الحلم".

كبر آدم وهو يرى مدينته محاصرة، يسمع أصوات الطائرات قبل أن ينام، ويستيقظ أحيانًا على أخبار فقدان جار أو قريب. ومع ذلك، بقي البحر ملاذه الأمن. كان يذهب إليه كلما ضاقت به الحياة، يسكب في مياهه همومه، ويعود محمّلًا بهدوء مؤقت، كمن يغتسل داخليًا.

الفصل الثاني: اللقاء

في أحد أيام الصيف، بينما كان يسير في السوق المزدحم، لمح فتاة تقف عند زاوية صغيرة تبيع كتبًا مستعملة. اقترب منها، فوقع نظره على كتاب عنوانه: "حين تحيا القلوب رغم الألم".

ابتسم وسألها:
- "أهذا كتابك؟"
ابتسمت بخجل وقالت:
- "لكنه يشبهني، فأنا أعيش الألم وأبحث عن حياة بين السطور ...ليتني كنت الكاتبة"

كان اسمها "سلمى"، فتاة في مثل عمره تقريبًا، عيناها تحملان بريقًا من الحزن والعزيمة معًا. منذ ذلك اليوم صار يلتقي بها أكثر، يتحدثان عن الكتب والأحلام، وكان كل لقاء بينهما نافذة ضوء وسط الظلام.

الفصل الثالث: تحت الحصار

كبرت صداقتهما سريعًا. كانا يجلسان على شاطئ البحر لساعات، تتحدث هي عن حلمها أن تصبح كاتبة مشهورة، ويخبرها هو عن دفاتره المليئة بالحكايات.

لكن الحصار كان حاضرًا في كل التفاصيل: انقطاع الكهرباء، قلة الماء، أصوات الطائرات.

كانت سلمى تقول:

"نحن نعيش بين قصفين، ومع ذلك نحاول أن نصنع حياة بينهما".

وكان آدم يرد مبتسمًا:

"إذن نحن أقوى من الموت، لأننا نحب رغم كل شيء".

الفصل الرابع: بدايات الحب

مع مرور الوقت، لم تعد لقاءاتهما مجرد حديث عن الكتب. كان بينهما شيء أعمق. نظرات طويلة، صمت دافئ، وقلوب تخفق رغم الخوف.

كتب آدم في دفتره:

"هي الحياة التي ···كلما التقيتها، شعرت أنني أقترب أكثر من نفسي. هي لست فقط سلمى، أبحث عنها".

الفصل الخامس: العاصفة

لكن في غزة، لا يستمر الصفاء طويلاً. ذات ليلة، دوّت أصوات الانفجارات، واشتعلت السماء بالنار.

ركض آدم نحو بيت سلمى بعد القصف، لكنه وجد الركام والدخان فقط. بحث عنها بين المستشفيات، بين وجوه اللاجئين، لكن لم يجدها.

لم يبقَ سوى دفتر صغير سقط من بين أنقاض البيت. فتحه بيدين مرتجفتين، فوجد على الصفحة الأخيرة جملة كتبتها:

"إذا لم نجد الحياة على الأرض، فربما نجدها بين الكلمات".

الفصل السادس: رحلة البحث

لم يستسلم آدم. لأيام طويلة، ظل يسأل عنها في كل مكان: عند أقاربها، في المستشفيات، عند مراكز الإغاثة.

كل إجابة كانت تزيد من خوفه، لكن قلبه كان يرفض أن يصدق أنها رحلت.

كتب في دفتره:

"سأبحث عنك يا سلمى، ولو بين الغيوم والدخان. أنتِ لم تكوني عابرة، بل كنتِ الوطن كله."

الفصل السابع: رسائل الدفتر

حين عاد إلى البحر، فتح دفتر سلمى وبدأ يقرأ رسائلها. وجده مليئًا بسطور كتبتها ولم تُره إياها:

«آدم، كنتَ صديقي حين احتجتُ، وأملي حين يئست، وأعلم أن كلماتي ستصل إليك حتى لو افترقنا».

كل جملة كانت كأنها نبض جديد في قلبه. شعر أن سلمى لم تمت، بل تعيش في الكلمات.

الفصل الثامن: الأمل والكتابة

جلس آدم عند البحر، حيث بدأ كل شيء، لكنه لم يكن حزينًا هذه المرة. أمسك قلمه وبدأ يكتب روايته الأولى.

كتب عن البحر الذي علّمه الصبر، عن سلمى التي علّمته الحب، عن غزة التي علمته المقاومة بالحياة قبل السلاح.

حين انتهى، أغلق دفتره وقال:

"إن تُمحى الحكايات ما دام هناك من يكتبها"

ورفع عينيه نحو السماء، التي رغم الغيوم، كانت تعد بميلاد شمس جديدة.

الخاتمة

تحت سماء غزة، يولد الحب رغم الموت، وتبقى الكلمات حين يرحل كل شيء.